W9-AYF-063

SPORTS ON THE EDGE!

EXTREME SURFING

STEVEN OTFINOSKI

Marshall Cavendish
Benchmark
New York

NOTE FROM THE PUBLISHER:
Do not attempt this sport without wearing proper safety gear and taking safety precautions.

Website: www.marshallcavendish.us

This publication represents the opinions and views of the author based on Steven Otfinoski's personal experience, knowledge, and research. The information in this book serves as a general guide only. The author and publisher have used their best efforts in preparing this book and disclaim liability rising directly and indirectly from the use and application of this book.

Other Marshall Cavendish Offices:
Marshall Cavendish International (Asia) Private Limited, 1 New Industrial Road, Singapore 536196 • Marshall Cavendish International (Thailand) Co Ltd. 253 Asoke, 12th Flr, Sukhumvit 21 Road, Klongtoey Nua, Wattana, Bangkok 10110, Thailand • Marshall Cavendish (Malaysia) Sdn Bhd, Times Subang, Lot 46, Subang Hi-Tech Industrial Park, Batu Tiga, 40000 Shah Alam, Selangor Darul Ehsan, Malaysia

Marshall Cavendish is a trademark of Times Publishing Limited

All websites were available and accurate when this book was sent to press.

LIBRARY OF CONGRESS CATALOGING-IN-PUBLICATION DATA
Otfinoski, Steven.
Extreme surfing / Steven Otfinoski.
p. cm. — (Sports on the edge!)
Includes bibliographical references and index.
Summary: "Explores sport of extreme surfing"—Provided by publisher.
ISBN 978-1-60870-231-2 (print) ISBN 978-1-60870-751-5 (ebook)
1. Surfing—Juvenile literature. 2. Extreme sports—Juvenile literature. I. Title.
GV839.55.O84 2012
797.3'2—dc22
2010028715

EDITOR: Christine Florie PUBLISHER: Michelle Bisson
ART DIRECTOR: Anahid Hamparian SERIES DESIGNER: Kristen Branch

EXPERT READER: Meg Bernardo, Executive Manager, Association of Surfing Professionals
North America, Huntington Beach, California

Photo research by Marybeth Kavanagh

Cover photo by Pierre Tostee/ASP/Getty Images
The photographs in this book are used by permission and through the courtesy of: *SuperStock:* Ron Dahlquist, 4; Flirt, 13; Blend Images, 14; *The Image Works:* Roger-Viollet, 6; *Getty Images:* Michael Ochs Archives, 9; Chris Dyball/Innerlight, 16; Cameron Spencer, 29; Chris Polk/WireImage, 30; Hulton Archive, 33; Karen Wilson/ASP, 34; Jim Russi/Covered Images/ASP, 40; *Alamy:* Nick Hanna, 10; Aurora Photos, 11; Mark A. Johnson, 25; *Landov:* Will Burgess/Reuters, 17; Victor Fraile/Reuters, 23; Jay Clarke/MCT, 38; *Newscom:* t13/ZUMA Press, 21; Pierre Tostee/ZUMA Press, 31; *Corbis:* Rick Doyle, 22; Karen Wilson/epa, 24

Printed in Malaysia (T)
1 3 5 6 4 2

Contents

ONE

SURFING— SPORT OF KINGS

FEW EXPERIENCES ARE AS thrilling as riding the **curl** of a wave on a surfboard. Since the 1960s, surfing has captured the imagination of many; and a whole subculture has grown up around it, with its own fashions, music, and movies.

Surfing is the granddaddy of extreme sports. Without surfing there would be no skateboarding

← WHETHER CATCHING THE PERFECT WAVE FOR A LONG RIDE OR FOR PERFORMING HEART-STOPPING TRICKS, IT'S NO WONDER THAT SURFING IS ONE OF THE MOST POPULAR SPORTS IN THE WORLD.

or snowboarding. While surfing is an ancient sport, once pursued by kings of the South Pacific islands, it has only become popular in the United States in the last hundred years.

Hawaii Leads the Way

Surfing originated in the islands of Polynesia in the South Pacific Ocean in ancient times. It was especially

EARLY HAWAIIANS RODE THE WAVES EITHER BY LYING DOWN OR STANDING ON LONG, WOODEN BOARDS.

popular in the Hawaiian Islands, where it was not just a sport but an important part of native culture and religion. The Hawaiians called it *he'e nalu* (hay-eh na-loo), which in English means "wave sliding."

Among the first Europeans to observe surfing were English explorer Captain James Cook and his crew, who arrived in Hawaii in 1778. "The boldness and address [direction of energy] with which they [the surfers] performed was altogether astonishing," wrote one crew member in his journal.

European missionaries arrived in Hawaii in the early 1800s and frowned on many native customs, including surfing. In 1821 they banned the sport. By the start of the 1900s surfing had all but disappeared in the land that gave birth to it.

The Rebirth of Surfing

In the early 1900s a few hardy Hawaiians rediscovered surfing and again began riding the waves on Waikiki Beach in Honolulu. One of these pioneers was George Freeth, who was of Hawaiian and Irish ancestry.

In 1907 railroad tycoon Henry Huntington hired Freeth to come to California to demonstrate surfing at Redondo Beach. It was a publicity stunt to attract people to travel from Los Angeles to Redondo Beach on Huntington's new railroad. Californians were thrilled watching Freeth surf, and he continued his demonstrations up and down the coast, attracting newcomers to the sport.

In 1912 surfer James "Big Jim" Matthias Jordan Jr. demonstrated surfing at Virginia Beach, Virginia. Virginia Beach became the center of surfing on the East Coast of the United States and remains so today.

Surfing's Golden Age

Through the 1950s surfing remained a sport with a loyal, but small, following. Then in the 1960s, movies and pop music celebrating surfing helped to make it popular among young people. Singing groups such as the Beach Boys and instrumental groups such as Dick Dale and the Del-Tones and the Surfaris had hit record after hit record that celebrated surfing and the carefree lifestyle of surfers. Surfing was also highlighted in popular teen films such as *Gidget* and in a series of beach movies starring Annette Funicello and Frankie Avalon. However, real surfers found those films silly and unrealistic.

The first film to show real surfers surfing was the documentary *Endless Summer* (1966) directed by Bruce Brown. Brown and his film crew followed surfers Mike Hynson and Robert August around the world as they searched for the perfect wave. The film cost only $50,000 to produce and grossed more than $20 million at the box office.

In the 1980s surfers were traveling the world looking for bigger waves. They found them along the coasts of Hawaii, South America, and northern

THE BEACH BOYS' SURFIN' SAFARI ALBUM COVER FROM 1962 IS A GOOD EXAMPLE OF THE CALIFORNIA SURFER LIFESTYLE SO COMMONLY PORTRAYED AT THAT TIME.

EVOLUTION OF THE SURFBOARD

NEW TECHNOLOGY ALSO contributed to surfing's golden age. For decades surfboards were big, made of heavy wood, and difficult to transport. Then in 1949 Californian Bob Simmons built the first successful fiberglass surfboard. He called it the "sandwich," and it was made of a Styrofoam core, a thin layer of plywood, and an outer coating of fiberglass. Simmons's boards were smaller, lighter, and easier to carry than traditional surfboards. He drove up and down the California coast in a beat-up car selling his boards to surfers. In 1958 Hobart "Hobie" Alter and Gordon Clark improved on the fiberglass board, giving it a foam core of polyurethane, which made it even lighter.

A SURFER CLEARS THE BREAK OF A 70-FOOT WAVE AT MAVERICK'S BEACH AT HALF MOON BAY IN CALIFORNIA.

California at Maverick's Beach, where the waves reached heights of 30 to 50 feet. Surfing these massive waves required a boldness and skill unseen since the days of the early Hawaiians. Surfers developed new moves and tricks to challenge themselves. Professional surfers used these tricks to win the growing number of national and international surfing competitions. A new age of extreme surfing was born.

READY, SET, SURF!

TWO

AS WITH ANY EXTREME sport, becoming skillful at surfing, takes hard work, patience, and care. If you've never surfed before, try bodysurfing first. Go into the water and watch the waves wash up on the beach. Put yourself in the water facing the shore and then dive in when a wave breaks over you. Let the power of the wave pull you. You can try this with a bodyboard or a rubber air mattress, too. Soon you'll get a feel for the ocean and gain a respect for its awesome power.

TO GET THE FEEL OF THE WAVES AND WATER, TRY RIDING ON A BODYBOARD BEFORE HITTING THE WAVES ON A SURFBOARD.

ESSENTIAL EQUIPMENT

Okay, now you're ready to get yourself a surfboard, the most essential equipment for every surfer. There are two basic kinds of boards: long boards and short boards. As a beginner, you'll probably want to start with a long board. Most long boards are at least 9 feet long and have a wide, long **nose**, or front part.

LONG BOARDS (LEFT AND CENTER) ARE GOOD
FOR BEGINNERS. SHORT BOARDS (RIGHT) ARE FOR
THOSE WITH MORE EXPERIENCE.

Long boards are very stable and give a long, graceful ride. Short boards range from 5 to 8 feet in length and have a narrow **nose**. They have greater maneuverability than long boards, but it takes more skill to stay on them. Short boards are favored by more experienced surfers who want to perform daring tricks and stunts.

When choosing a surfboard, look for one that is at least as tall as your hand stretched above your head. It should also fit under your arm for easy carrying.

A **wet suit** is quickly becoming another piece of essential equipment for most surfers. The wet suit is a tight-fitting outfit that covers your body and is made of a thin, synthetic rubber called neoprene. Wearing a wet suit allows you to keep warm in the water and stay there for a longer time. The suit actually allows a thin layer of water to penetrate it. The water is warmed by your body heat in the same way that a hot water bottle keeps you warm when pressed against your skin. When surfing in rocky waters, rubber booties will help to protect your feet from being cut by rocks and shells.

Wipeout!

WHEN YOU wipe out, you fall off your surfboard. This happens to every surfer on a regular basis, so don't feel bad. When falling, keep your body as parallel as possible to the water's surface. This way you won't hit the bottom in shallow water. Cover your head with your arms to protect it from being hit by your surfboard. Then, as you rise to the water's surface, keep your arms above your head again to avoid being hit by the board, which should be attached to your ankle by a leash.

A SURFER LEAVES THE WATER TETHERED TO HIS BOARD WITH A LEASH.

A **leash** is a plastic cord that connects you to your surfboard. It stretches from the **tail**, or back end of the board, to the ankle of one foot. The leash serves two purposes. It keeps you from losing your board in the water when you fall off, and it protects other surfers and swimmers from being clobbered and possibly injured by your loose surfboard when you do fall.

Surfing wax is a sticky substance to rub on the top of your board to help prevent your feet from slipping when standing on it.

That's the bare basics of surfing. Don't get discouraged if you have trouble getting up on the board or wipe out time after time. Surfing is a skill that takes lots of time and practice. Think about taking lessons with a qualified instructor. You'll learn more quickly and more safely that way.

THE FOUR Ps:
A QUICK BEGINNER'S GUIDE TO SURFING

Paddle out to the waves. Enter the water with your board and lie on it, chest down. Use your arms to paddle to the waves with swift, even strokes. Keep your head up and your eyes on the horizon. Look for gently falling white water. Avoid big, crashing waves.

Push through any oncoming waves with both hands holding onto the sides, or rails, of the surfboard.

Prepare yourself when you reach the breaking waves. Face the shore and push the nose of the board underneath the wave. Get one foot flat on the board and wait for the wave to come up on the board.

Pop up on the board with your feet in one flowing motion as you catch the wave. Keep one foot in front of the other to stabilize yourself on the board. For most surfers this is the left foot, or regular foot, but some prefer the right foot. That's called having a goofy foot.

19

WILD AND WET MOVES

WHEN SURFERS HARNESS the power of the ocean's waves, anything and everything is possible. Today's extreme surfers perform incredible moves and stunts on the waves, in the air, and while being towed behind a **Personal Watercraft (PWC)**.

Hanging Ten and More

When a surfer can "**hang ten**," that person knows he or she has arrived. Hanging ten is when you can curl all ten toes over the nose of your surfboard while in motion. It remains the most skillful move in long-board surfing.

20

IT'S CALLED "HANGING TEN" WHEN ALL TEN TOES CURL OVER THE FRONT TIP OF A SURFBOARD.

It requires perfect balance, careful timing, and a feel for the wave you're riding.

There are other tricks and stunts that surfers spend years mastering. Surfing "off the lip" is riding the board at the top part of the wave and coming off the crest. To "cut back" is to take the board toward the wave's highest point. That is where the greatest energy is given off by the wave. "Walking the board" is exactly what it sounds like: walking from the tail to the nose of the board while in motion.

THIS SURFER CUTS BACK OFF THE LIP OF A WAVE.

AERIAL SURFING

Both skateboarding and snowboarding evolved from surfing. Aerial surfing is derived from the airborne antics of these other two extreme sports. To defy gravity and go airborne, a surfer must find just the right wave. It must be a strong, vertical wave to provide the proper liftoff. Once the surfer has zeroed in on the wave, he or she must move toward the cresting wave as quickly as possible. Staying high in the pocket of the wave (the section ahead of the broken part of a wave) when it is steepest is essential. Once launched, the surfer must relax his or her body, especially the leg muscles, in a process known as "deweighting."

There are a number of aerial movements, most of them based on how the surfer grabs the board while in midair. There's the fronthand grab, the backhand grab, and the stale fish air, which consists of reaching behind to grab the tip of the leg's heel.

Traditional competitions did not allow aerial surfing for years; today it has become widely accepted. "That's the future of surfing," says top surfer Kelly Slater. "It's really in the air."

A SURFER LAUNCHES AN AERIAL OFF THE LIP OF A WAVE DURING THE QUIKSILVER PRO FRANCE COMPETITION.

THE RODEO CLOWN FLIP

THE MOST CHALLENGING aerial move of all is the rodeo clown flip, inspired by a rodeo stunt. The surfer grabs the board with both hands and does a complete back flip in the air before landing. It is so difficult that until recently, one of the only documented examples on video was performed by Aaron Cormican in 2000. In June 2009 Jordy Smith of South Africa performed a rodeo clown flip while practicing with the Red Bull surf team in the Mentawai Islands in Indonesia. That same month, American Patrick Gudauskas completed the first one in competition in the Maldives, an island chain in the Indian Ocean. In August 2009 Hawaiian surfer Matt Meola landed a rodeo clown flip in a competition on Maui, one of the Hawaiian islands.

A PILOT TOWS A SURFER DOWN A WAVE. THIS KIND OF SURFING IS EXTREMELY DANGEROUS AND SHOULD NOT BE PRACTICED BY BEGINNERS.

Tow-In Surfing

Perhaps the most radical and hottest kind of extreme surfing today is **tow-in surfing**. It resembles water skiing in that one surfer tows another by a line with a high-power PWC. The pilot steers for the waves and then releases the surfer, who takes off at a high speed. Later, the two surfers reverse positions.

Tow-in surfing can be dangerous and should be attempted *only* by adult, experienced surfers. Some surfers don't approve of this latest development in extreme surfing. They say it goes against the natural matching of surfer and waves by bringing a machine into the mix.

Safe Surfing

Whether you're a beginner, an experienced surfer, or a high-flying aerialist, there are safety rules you must follow.

Safety begins even before you get into the water. Choose a beach or area to surf in that is free of rocks and dangerous sea life, such as sharks. Observe the waves. They should be high and composed of white water, but not the kind of pounding surf that poses dangers. Check out the weather report before you head out. If the weather is stormy or the tides are unpredictable, wait for better weather.

Don't surf alone. Go out with a friend or a group. If you run into trouble in the water, there will be someone to help you. Finally, and perhaps most importantly, know how to swim. Swimming skills are critical when in deep water. You may float on your surfboard; but if you are separated from it, you'll need to be able to swim back to shore.

Here are some more safety "rules of the waves" to keep in mind when surfing:

1. BE READY. You must be prepared to think fast when riding a wave. For example, if you're caught inside a breaking wave and someone's board comes crashing toward you, dive down into the water to avoid being hit.

2. BE AWARE. Conditions in the water can change quickly. Keep an eye out for changing conditions, dangerous sea creatures such as eels or sharks, and the location of other surfers around you.

3. BE COURTEOUS. Be polite to other surfers, whether you know them or not. If someone surfing near you is closer to the peak of a wave, back off and let the other surfer take the wave. You'd want that person to do the same for you. To avoid running into other surfers, avoid crowded areas.

THE BIG KAHUNAS

SURFING HAS ITS top athletes and heroes just like every sport does. Professional surfers travel the world competing in top tournaments for big money on the **Association of Surfing Professionals (ASP)** World Tour. Here are a few of the "big **kahunas**" of the surfing world.

Surfing's Michael Jordan

U.S. surfer Kelly Slater (1972–) has been called "the Michael Jordan of professional surfing," and he has the awards to prove it. Slater has won the ASP World Championship record nine times. He is the

KELLY SLATER LEARNED TO SURF IN THE WAVES OFF OF COCOA BEACH, FLORIDA.

youngest surfer to win the title (at age twenty) and the oldest (at age thirty-six) in 2008. In 2009, at an age when many surfers are past their prime, he ranked sixth in the world.

A fierce competitor on his surfboard, Slater has many other interests. He has been a professional actor on television and in movies, plays guitar in his own surf band, and has written two books.

DANE REYNOLDS—BEST OF THE NEW BREED

If Kelly Slater stands for surfing's proud past and present, Dane Reynolds (1985–) represents its exciting future. This radical young surfer from Ventura, California, is known for taking risks every time he enters a competition. Reynolds scored the highest for single-wave events at both the 2003 and 2004 **X Games**. His amazing back-to-back aerials helped him to be named ASP's Rookie of the Year in 2008. Despite his bold and daring moves in tournaments, Reynolds is humble and shy when he's not catching a wave on his surfboard.

DANE REYNOLDS SURFS DURING THE 2004 X GAMES IN HUNTINGTON BEACH, CALIFORNIA.

BROTHERS BRUCE (LEFT) AND ANDY (RIGHT) IRONS
WERE A FORCE TO BE RECKONED WITH AT THE 2005
RIP CURL PRO PIPELINE MASTERS IN OAHU, HAWAII.

THE IRONS BROTHERS

Brother acts are rare in any sport; and in surfing, Andy
and Bruce Irons were the outstanding example. Born
in Hawaii about a year apart, the brothers were among
the elite in professional surfing. They were best known
for speed surfing and their fresh and original tricks
and moves. Bruce Irons (1979–) is famous for his

radical aerial stunts. He beat Kelly Slater to win the 2001 Pipe Masters event and won the Rip Curl Pro Search 2008 in Indonesia. Brother Andy (1978–2010) took the Rip Curl Pro Search title in 2006 and 2007. He was also the star of a surfing documentary called *Blue Horizon* (2004). The brothers and their family host the Annual Irons Brothers Pinetrees Classic for young surfers on the north shore of the Hawaiian island of Kauai.

Make Way for the Women

Few women surfed until Margo Godfrey Oberg (1953–) won the 1968 World Contest for women at age fifteen and became a role model. She proved to be as graceful on a surfboard as any man, but retired in 1972 after marrying Steve Oberg. Margo returned to surfing three years later. Margo is the first professional women's world champion, crowned in 1977. She won the ASP World Champion title again in 1980 and 1981. Today she runs the Margo Oberg Surfing School on Poipu Beach on Kauai, which she opened in 1977.

DUKE KAHANAMOKU — FATHER OF MODERN SURFING

PERHAPS NO ONE has done more to promote the sport of surfing in modern times than Duke Kahanamoku. Born in Hawaii, he was one of nine children of a police officer in Honolulu. He grew up surfing on Waikiki Beach with his brothers. An expert swimmer and lifeguard, Duke entered the 1912 Olympics and won a gold medal in swimming. He won two more Olympic medals for swimming, in 1920 and 1924.

But it was Duke's daring demonstrations of surfing in California, on the East Coast, and in Australia that captured the imagination of millions of people. In 1965 he hosted the first Duke Kahanamoku Invitational on the Hawaiian island of Oahu, the big-wave event of its day. Duke served as Hawaii's official greeter in his last years. *Surfing* magazine named him the century's most influential surfer in 1999.

SERENA BROOKE COMPETES IN THE 2005 SPC
FRUIT PRO EVENT AT BELLS BEACH, AUSTRALIA.

Australian Serena Brooke (1976–) first appeared on the international surf scene in 1990 when she was fourteen. She turned pro after graduating from high school and ranked fifth in the world in women's surfing in 2001. A popular figure in surfing, Brooke starred in a surfing documentary, has her own fitness video, holds surfing camps for children, and runs the Serena Brooke Charity Foundation in Huntington Beach, California.

FIVE

BIG WAVES, BIG WINNERS

PROFESSIONAL SURFERS TRAVEL the world to compete in major tournaments and big-wave events. Yet the ultimate extreme sport has had a troubled history at the premier event for extreme sports, the X Games.

Surfing at the X Games

The X Games were started by the Entertainment Sports Programming Network (ESPN) in 1995. Surfing was not a category in the games, however, until 2003. The first two years, the surfing competitions were held at Huntington Beach Pier in California. While the competitions were well documented, they were, in the words of one enthusiast, "very un-extreme events." The surfers were world-class, but the surf itself was less so. In 2005, at the insistence of world surfing officials, the X Games' surfing competition was moved to Zicatela Beach in Puerto Escondido, Mexico, where the waves were bigger and more challenging. The only problem was that the rest of the Summer X Games were held in Los Angeles, where they could be broadcast live. Without live coverage, the surfing competitions were not widely seen and had trouble getting sponsorship.

After much deliberation, the organizers of the X Games dropped surfing from its list of events in 2008. The schedule overlapped with a major surfing competition event in South Africa, the Association of Surfing Professionals—World Championship Tour, where most of the top surfing pros were competing. The X Games organizers said they would reevaluate the surfing competition, but in 2009 it again was not included in the games.

ARTIFICIAL WAVES

UNTIL RECENTLY, if you wanted to surf in the United States, you had to go to one coast or the other. Now, though, artificial wave surf environments exist across the country. The first artificial surfing reef in the United States, Pratte's Reef, was created in El Segundo, California, in 1999. It was composed of 14-ton sandbags in a wedge formation. However, the reef failed after only a few years when the sandbags broke. More successful was the FlowRider (left), invented by surfer Tom Lochtefeld. The FlowRider is a large, fiberglass pool-like surfing environment that uses water pumps to thrust 100,000 gallons of water per minute and create a sheet 2 inches thick that flows over a foam-padded surface. The rider slides down a ramp on a special surfboard and into the curl of the wave. The first FlowRider was built for a water park in New Braunfels, Texas, in 2000. Today there are more than one hundred FlowRider installations around the world in water parks and hotels, and on board cruise ships. Before you run out to buy one for your backyard, however, you should know that a FlowRider costs $1 million and up!

A SURFER COMPETES AT THE 2006 VAN'S TRIPLE CROWN IN OAHU, HAWAII.

SURFING'S TRIPLE CROWN

One of the biggest annual events in surfing competition is actually six events in one. The Van's Triple Crown is held on Oahu's north shore. Men and women compete in separate tournaments at Haleiwa Ali'i Beach Park, Sunset Beach, and the Banzai Pipeline. The sixth event—the women's Billabong Pro Maui—is held in Honolulu Bay on Maui. In the triple crown, begun in 1983, the world's best surfers compete at three unique locations, each with its own challenges. Waves on the north shore reach a height of 50 feet.

OTHER BIG EVENTS

The Mormaii Pe'ahi Tow-In World Cup Championship is one of the world's few tow-in big-wave contests. It was first held in January 2002 on Maui, and in 2008 it took place at Punta de Lobos, Chile. The Association of Professional Towsurfers (APT), founded in 2003, also has a tour. One of the most popular contests in California is the Quiksilver "Men Who Ride Mountains" Big Wave Event held at Maverick's Beach in Half Moon Bay near San Francisco. Only those top surfers who are invited may compete; and if the waves aren't big enough, the event is postponed until the next year.

Surfing, the original extreme sport, continues to be popular around the world. No other sport pits an athlete's skill and endurance against the forces of nature so dramatically. It is a challenge surfers can't resist in their quest for the perfect wave.

GLOSSARY

Association of Surfing Professionals (ASP) the governing body of world professional surfing

curl the curve that forms as the top of a wave breaks

goofy foot the natural preference for bringing the right foot forward when surfing

hang ten placing all ten toes over the nose of a moving surfboard

kahuna an expert surfer; originally a Hawaiian priest or wizard

leash a plastic cord that connects the surfer's body with his or her surfboard

nose the first 12 inches of the surfboard

Personal Watercraft (PWC) a recreational water craft that a person rides in while standing or sitting

rails the sides of a surfboard

regular foot the natural preference for bringing the left foot forward when surfing

tail the back end of a surfboard

tow-in surfing a kind of extreme surfing where one person tows a surfer with a Personal Watercraft at high speed, similar to water skiing

wet suit a tight-fitting outfit made of synthetic rubber worn by a surfer

white water the broken part of a wave that has peaked

wipe out to fall off a surfboard

X Games annual sporting event involving various extreme-action games, such as skateboarding and snowboarding

FIND OUT MORE

BOOKS

Crowe, Ellie. *Surfer of the Century: The Life of Duke Kahanamoku.* New York: Lee & Low Books, 2007.

Fitzpatrick, Jim. *Surfing* (Healthy for Life). Ann Arbor, MI: Cherry Lake Publishing, 2007.

Haber, Quinn. *Experience Pipeline.* San Diego: Casagrande Press, 2008.

McFee, Shane. *Surfing* (Living on the Edge). New York: PowerKids Press, 2008.

Sandler, Michael. *Super Surfers* (X-Moves). New York: Bearport Publishing, 2009.

DVDs

Bustin' Down the Door. Screen Media, 2009.

Classic Surf Films. Topics Entertainment, 2008.

Step Into Liquid. Lionsgate Home Entertainment, 2008.

ABC of Surfing

www.abc-of-surfing.com

This site contains numerous articles on surfing basics and information, as well as news, pictures, and forums.

All Star Activities—Surfing

www.allstaractivities.com/sports/surfing

This site provides useful information on all aspects of surfing, from the sport's history to buying a used surfboard.

Surfing Information

www.gumbylock.com.au/Aussie/html/Rules.html

Detailed information on surfing etiquette and rules, safety tips, and much more.

INDEX

Page numbers in **boldface** are illustrations.

ABOUT THE AUTHOR

STEVEN OTFINOSKI has published 145 books for young readers, including more than two dozen biographies and books about animals, history, and states for Marshall Cavendish. He lives in Connecticut with his wife Beverly, an English teacher and editor, and their two children.